DREAM CATCHER

An old man's dreams and observations of life.

By

EDDIE J MARTIN

CONTENTS

1

AN OLD MAN

To: Our Senior Citizens.

Many Events occur in the world of the seniors, just ask one!

YOU SEE SOME of the weirdest people when you're out in the park, people that you never expect to see together are together. There is a short little fellow, plain, bowlegged with a beard of about 35 years old with a younger girl of say 19 and gorgeous. You wonder what this guy is got that this young lady sees in him. I never could understand that. Or there is this huge woman of about 6 feet 2, 275 pounds with this small man of say 5 foot 2 and one hundred and 45 pounds. What in the hell could he do for her, he'd need a step ladder to climb up on top of her.

You see all kinds in the park, just sit, watch and listen. And then there's the cell phones, parents in the park with their kids for an outing, the kids wanting to play and they're telling them to go away "can't you see I'm on the phone". Can't attend to their kids for talking on that damn cell phone. Mothers can't push the babies in their strollers for talking on that cell phone. People walk into each other while "you guessed it "talking on their cell phones. Telephone poles, pools, walking over people while there laying on the lawn. Believe me it's hilarious. The park bench is a good place to see it all, front row seat, and don't forget to bring your camera.

Prologue

She walked through the service station area and had no idea anyone was watching every step she took. Watching every movement she made, everything about her from the scarf on her head to the ear rings she wore to the necklace around her neck. The shameless halter she wore cut off at the Naval to the shorts hung low on the butt and cut off at the Crouch. The tattoo of a willow tree on her right thigh and a rainbow on her left. Someone's name above her left breast and a star on her right. A roses on her ankle along with the ankle chain. She never knew someone was watching but then again I'll bet she was hoping. No worries my love, I'm watching.

The jet flew overhead, the airstream streaking behind. I'm in the pilot seat telling the copilot to take the

controls because I'm going to take a little snooze. Wake me when we get to Phoenix.

AN OLD MAN of about 72 was walking in the park, at a leisurely pace, cane in his left hand, just cooling it. Probably thinking about his past, all the things he's done in his life, right and wrong. The women he's met…And he smiles to himself and wonders would he do it all again if he had the chance, would he change anything? The answer is always yes, and no but life has been good.

What goes through a person's mind, I mean short of dreaming. What is he thinking, Say a man of between 70 and 80, who lived his life and has his leisure time ahead just to do nothing. Does he think of his past or does he see the present in the same light as someone younger than he. Or does he look toward the future. I think the present may be more Interesting, for instance that lady there, I wonder what's her story. She walks in this library like she have more on her mind then books. She's about 28 years old, a little heavy I'd say but cute. I'm sure she would have no trouble finding a man, if there were troubles with her it would probably be about men it usually is. I would even say she has a kid or two, I've learned if a woman has an ass that is spread kind of wide like hers then she has kids. She set at a desk and put her books down but didn't open them, just sat there and looked straight ahead. Now I wonder what's on her mind.

2

Doris and Me

I TRIED TO do the right thing Honest I have but it seemed as though life never goes my way, it shouldn't be that way because I have a nice home, two automobiles, a very nice husband and two Lovely kids. I got everything I ever wanted much more than my mother ever had. Dad always beat on her until she didn't know if she was coming or going. She was always afraid of him and then there we were in the middle. Eventually my mother said to hell with it and left all of us. Dad, the three kids and the two dogs. In our teen's dad died an alcoholic and regretting what he had done to run mom off.

My life is nothing like that, I've got a husband that wouldn't ever think about striking me. My kids are as nice as could be, 3 and 6-year-olds always with the yes ma'am and no ma'am thing. So what is it, am I going through the changes at 28. It seems like every time I pass another of the same sex I stare at them, well not really but it seems like I'm staring at them. You know if it was a male it wouldn't be as bad but it's a female. It started about a year ago at a house party one of the neighbors gave. Naturally everyone was drinking, dancing and having a good time like all parties. And we were all kind of intoxicated. Since all of us lived in the neighborhood and no one had to drive everyone felt it was okay. I guess everyone felt it was more than okay to drink a little more than usual. At first I put it on to the drinking to what happened but then I started thinking about it and thereafter. My neighbor from six houses down a black haired woman of about 32, midsize and quite cute, somehow we ended up in the coat room together or one of the bedrooms that held the coats. Looking for ours before we left. The whole night we had been running into each other, I thought by accident but now I think not.

There were touching each other when there were no need for it, hugging each other and the small kiss on the cheeks. Some would say ladies do that kind of thing especially at parties but after I thought about it, I don't think so. Especially after what happened in the coat room. While looking for our coats, stumbling around we both fell on the bed and got all tangled up in coats by the time we found ourselves clear we were facing each other and lips being no more than 3 inches apart. We looked at each other and the next moment we found ourselves kissing. It was only a second but it felt like forever.

We looked at each other Embarrassed, I was anyway. Found our coats, retrieved our husbands and left. It was a month later when I saw Doris (let's call her that) at the local CVS drugstore, we acknowledged each other and when we passed in the aisle I noticed she glanced back at me and me her. Two aisles around I ran into her again and she stopped. Brenda, why don't we have coffee sometime, after all it's a shame we don't get together more often and we're just right down the street from each other. You're right I said why not, name a date. Do I have your phone number, I said? It started from there, coffee in the mornings after our kids were off to school, and husbands were off to work so we had the whole mornings to ourselves. Eventually we made it to the bedroom some time at my house and sometimes at hers. The one time we got a scare was when one of the other ladies wanted to join us, that lasted for about 3 weeks and then she got herself a job. We never stopped what we were doing we just had to rework our schedule. There came a time when Doris and I was spending more and more time together, shopping, shows, walks and once my husband asked me jokingly about it and I told him (don't you want me to have any friends?) He never brought it up again. My youngest was home from school sick one day and walked in on us kissing and he asked what we were doing and I said, saying goodbye. That's the way grown-ups say goodbye to each other. Kids take what you tell them as gospel! Then one day, a week ago now. Doris tells me that she loves me and wants to run away with me. Believe it or not I wasn't shocked at what she said nor offended. I felt the same.

Except I wouldn't say it out loud and she would definitely have to bring it up first. Neither one of us brought up husbands or kids, homes nor anything like that. We felt that one car a few cloths and we're off. The only reason I'm here at the library is to give it one last thought to see if I really want to do this. I really love Doris, they say if you love someone then take it to the top and the hell with everyone else. Tomorrow while the husbands are at work and the kids in school, we'll leave then. Yes, we'll leave then.

One never knows what's going through a person's mind or what's happening in their life, are they happy, sad. Are they having married problems, one never knows. Like the young lady I see on my walks every day she always says good morning but when I look at her I just wonder. What's bothering you today?

That bastard, I know he's doing something, he never came home last night. I got no excuses just business as usual from him. James, have you got somebody else I'd say? He hasn't answered me yet. He text me from work the other day and said he was taking me out to dinner, for me to get dressed, I felt kind of happy about that, we Haden been out in some time. I put on one of my best dresses, heels and necklace. I looked in the mirror and felt I was looking okay and that he would approve. He was supposed to pick me up at 8 PM. 8 turn into 9 and 9 turn into 10 and 11. He finally showed up at 2 in the morning. Of course I had long since undressed and gone to bed. The next morning I asked him what happened to him, shouldn't have asked that. He threw his coffee cup down and asked me why was I asking him shit like that, I had things on my mind and didn't feel like going anyplace. This has been going on for weeks now so this morning I asked him again has he got somebody else, just tell me. You see I had been hearing rumors about him being seen with another woman, I was just trying to get him to say one way or the other. Just tell me I said and we can go our separate ways. He kept staying out more and more and the day he called me a bitch and stormed out the house did it for me. My first stop was the bank, the joint bank account. I took 95% of the balance, only leaving enough for the mortgage. My savings account, money market and Christmas fund, I closed that and open it up at another bank. All my direct deposit I rerouted to the new bank. He never asked me about the money and why I closed the accounts but he knew. A couple of days after I did this he had the nerve to ask me for sex. I had to bite my tongue for what I really wanted to tell him. After going through this a few more days and me asking him about another woman he finally admitted it. Now, he moved out and I'm pondering what to do next. The running every morning is the only thing that seem to clear my mind but now I'm sleeping better than I ever have. I've got a feeling I'm going to be just fine.

Every person that walks the streets has a story to tell, if you could only read their minds. The kid that's riding those skateboards, bikes and skates. From 8 to 80 all have a story, I'm sure of it. The mothers, fathers, sisters and big brothers that drop them off at the park. Some more interesting than others.

Like The fellows in the Honda Civic over there, about 16 and 18 years old just sitting there smoking pot I guess. I wonder what their story is:

There late Garcia said to Juan. The 18 year old sitting on the passenger side. Give them time they'll be here. Then he turned up the CD player to El Lobo.

The 2nd joint of the morning they shared and they were feeling great. They had about a pound of weed and they were to meet two old boys that were to purchase it off them for a great price. . Garcia didn't want to go for it because he said the price was too good and you know what they say, if it's too good to be true… Juan was the oldest but Garcia was and has always been the most logical. If it wasn't for the girls telling them to do it and how much money could be made they wouldn't be here. I think we should wait another five minutes and then hit the road, Garcia said. Relax Juan said, and handed him the joint and said take a hit. The plan was to purchase five more pounds of pot and sale that and then buy ten more pounds and eventually go big time from there.

Juan thoughts were on a new ride after selling the grass, maybe a new Chevy Malibu. Nice wheels and the latest stereo equipment. In car phone and hidden place for his own private stash. Yeah, that's what he wanted. On the other hand Garcia was looking further ahead. The car was only a stepping stone, he was looking toward that first yacht and that first Learjet after that. Fuck that small stuff, Garcia was thinking big even at that tender age of 16.

Look there, Garcia said to Juan, isn't that your Buick coming into the park? Look like it Juan said. Now, what the hell is she doing here? Juan car drove around the park and they followed it with their eyes, eventually they spotted Garcia's Honda and they headed for it.

Juan's girlfriend who was driving looked over at him and smiled, have you sold the stuff yet she said. Juan looked over at her disgusted and couldn't hold himself. Jumped out of Garcia's car over to his own and snatched his girlfriend out and started beating on her. After knocking her to the ground he started kicking her asking her what the fuck was she doing there when she knew they were taking care of business. He started to take out his pistol and shoot the bitch but thought better of it.

Garcia just looked at his girl and she dropped low in the seat, he knew that was the end for him and that bitch. For someone to be as stupid as that and a home girl to... Regardless, that's no excuse.

That bitch is history. After Juan got finish kicking his girl's ass he told her to leave the park, like now!

He'll get with her when he gets back home. As the girls were leaving two men drove by in an old-school Chevy. They didn't stop just drove by and looked at them and kept going. They had seen what went down and wanted no parts of it. Two minutes later three cop cars came and parked on both side of them and one directly behind.

They were asked to step out the car and were searched. A roach was found in Juan pocket and pipe in Garcia's. The cops asked if they could search the car, Garcia said no, they searched anyway. They found the pound of pot and informed them that they were both under arrest. Look like we acquired ourselves a nice Honda said one officer to the other.

The things you see if you open your eyes, you can be anywhere just keep your eyes and your mind open. The mind is a beautiful thing. Uh, uh, here comes another one.

Marshall why did you followed me out here, there is no way you're going to convince me to give you that kind of money. I need that money for my retirement. Look here I' am telling you, if you give me this money I'll make that money you give me into three times the amount. All you have to do is get over that fear you have, There is your grandchildren that you could do much more for and God forbid you were to pass away, they'd have money left for their children. I know you'd want that. If you don't want to give up the full amount then just give half, I can do just as well with half. I'll tell you what give me a 4th, see how that works out for you and then put in another 4th, wait out a little while and put in another. Now you can't beat that, now you have to admit that right, right? How long have I been your advisor? You're acting like you don't trust me. I've only your best in mind. The day I put you in the wrong investment is the day I quit the business. You've seen the status report on the progress of that stocks, why want you believe that?

Marshall, it's hard to believe a newspaper name peekaboo business report. I need something more credible than that. Besides this is not the 1st time you come up with "sure things".

This time is different Marshall said. The longer you put it off the more money you losing.

Aren't you hot out here in that suit, tie and dress shoes? You're sweating like a pig.

Okay, okay what about this, how about me writing you a promissory note that should prove I'm on the up and up. I'm telling you you're missing out. I'm meeting with the board this afternoon to commit and purchase shares, I need your funds and commitment before then.

Okay Marshall I'm convinced, I'll let you have 10% of my retirement for investments, if it does well I'll let you have another 20%, that's all I'm doing.

Now, go away!

Thanks mom!

LITTLE KIDS WILL talk to anybody, say anything. Just let them talk and you listen, they say some of the damnedest things. The younger they are the more outrageous they sound.

Hi, who are you? My name is Ronnie and I'm 5 years old. I like ice cream, not too much candy but I like caramel. Your beard is so long, your hair is so gray. I've got a bike but I haven't learned to ride it yet, my parents bring it to the park so I could learn but I don't want to. Is sissy better than me? You know Mr., grades don't matter. My mommy and daddy do drugs, do tattoos hurt? Mommy and daddy are always talking about government. I like staying in my house watching TV and tipping in on my mama and daddy while there in the bedroom thinking I'm asleep. When I go in there room they don't even know I'm there. They are playing games and guess what? They play with no clothes on, they won't let me do that. My mama and daddy play leap frog, I wanted to play but they got mad and told me to go to bed. Made me mad!

I went to my big sister room and she was playing to, hide and seek she said. Some boy was going out the window with his pants only in one leg that was funny. My sister got mad! When everyone was sleep I went outside looking for my cat. I saw Mr. Wilson coming out the back door of the McDonnell's house and guess what Mr., Mrs. McDonnell kissed him before he left. He saw me and I waved at him. "Hi Mr. Wilson," I said. And guess what Mr., he put his finger over his lips and told me to Shhhh. Know what, I put my finger over my lips and told him to Shhhh. We have some crazy people around my house. A police car was in the alley one night when I let the dog out, I didn't see no police man so I peeked through the window and there he was in the back seat with his pants down and Susie leaning over him. I don't know what they were doing but when the policeman saw me he jumped up and asked me what was I doing up so late? I told him I was letting the dog out, what you doing? Oh I'm just helping the little lady find an ear ring she lost, he said, now get on back in your house. I won't to help find the ear ring I said. Git, he said.

Mr. I stay in a crazy neighborhood.

Ronnie, Ronnie, where are you? You get back here right now. Well I have to go Mr., my mom's calling.

You know what Mr., you don't talk very much do you?

3

THE SERVICE MAN

A service man and his girl walked by and it took me back to when I wore my uniform. I always received the utmost respect. Respect when I wore it even being black, I never had any problems with the police anyway. Maybe it's just me but sixty years later it's the same when I wear my hat with the service affiliation on it today. I notice the difference with and without the hat.

My mother and I was in downtown Detroit and had to ask for directions and there was a policeman nearby so I told her I would ask him. My mother said you should have worn your uniform, no I said it'll be all right. When I came back and told her of the negative reaction I received from the officer all she said was" I told you to wear your uniform "I'm thinking mom knew something that I didn't because turns out she was right.

There is something about the uniform that I guess I never wanted to believe but you do get respect when you wear it. For me it worked yesterday and it's working today.

The beauty of the park is the people, from all walks of life. All nationalities and for a time they all seem to get along. The walkers and runners, the runners some of them anyway fast, fast. Where they going that fast? The walkers are moving fast enough, going past me anyway. There was an old lady in a wheelchair that passed me, I wanted to grab her with my cane and say "hold on their sister, where you going." I don't know maybe it's my age I just don't see where everyone going in such a hurry. What happens once they get there? Then they run to get to someplace else. I guess no one has time to people watch, except me.

I pass by a sign that the city puts up that Says no alcohol, no smoking, no this or no that in the park. I think most people adhered to the posted signs but then there is those that look the other way and does it anyway. Once I saw a lady throw a piece of trash on the ground when a trash receptacle was close by. I just looked at her and thought this lady is about my age, she should know better. The youngsters you can give them a break because of their age but believe it or not they don't do it very much either. They will drink their beer though, pour the contents into a Coke container thinking they're fooling someone. That's what my generation used to do. Today they smoke the pot, I guess they can hide that a little better.

Hey pop! You talking to me young man I said. Yeah, said the kid, me and my girl has a question for you. How old do you have to be before you stop enjoying sex? I have no idea young man you would have to ask someone a lot older than me. How old are you pop? I'm 74 years old. And you're still having sex? That's what I'm telling you, I said. The girl beside him said, see I told you so. So you have no excuse. My uncle was having sex until he was 86 and the only reason he stopped then was because he died.

You mean to tell me you can still get it up pop? You getting awful personal young man but yes with a little help from my friends. You mean Viagra right? You are a very astute young man, are you having problems in that department? You're kind of young for that, I said. He just don't like to do it when I won't his girls said. I think I may find me somebody else. Look Georgia I do it enough just not enough for you. Well surmise to say I'm the one you need to satisfy, you need to ask the old man for some of his Viagra. I don't need no damn Viagra I'm just having a little setback. Talk to the old man maybe he can help a 22-year-old boy like you, I'm leaving.

Look old man I didn't want to tell you while she was here but I do need a little help, do you have any advice for me.

I don't know young man I think it's all in your head. We old guys used to just get ourselves a half pint of gin and keep going.

Today you have so many things going on you have no time to stop and smell the roses. Advice! The only advice I can give you is when it comes time to having sex with your partner you should thank of nothing else, your mind must be on nothing else but the drawls, the drawls and the drawls.

Your mind must be blank to everything else, only concentrating on your mate. Not how your ball club is doing, who won the boxing match the night before, even how your mother's operation turned out. Your job is the drawls, remember that. For right now go fetch your girl, run down to the liquor store and purchase yourself a half pint of gin and get busy. What about the Viagra pop, the boy said.

Get your own, I said.

Old man's advice:

Old man what do you know about love, just because you're old don't mean you're an authority. That's true I said but I do know one thing, there will only be one true love in your life and after that's finish there won't be another.

It will go all the way of that 1st kiss, that 1st orgasm, in the case of the girl that 1st and only cherry. They only get the one, you can't get it back. There will be forever and always that 1st love, you will always remember and cherish. There is a lot of kids in the park and some will show us old men little or no respect. Like some would say" hey old man how long did it take you to get that old?" I'll bet you're older than Mount Fuji. Things like that. Kinda wonder what the younger generation coming to, then you meet the kid that comes up to you and say "old man, when I grow up I want to have as much knowledge as you. Then you have renewed faith in the children because you know someone got it.

I don't get upset when the kids say things like that to me because I remember saying the same thing to the generation before me. I use to ask them "old man "how many girls have you had and tell me should I have only one or one at a time. Should I stay in my race or venture out? Should I date ugly girls are try for the pretty girls all the time. Often girls? Are girls all that? You're full of questions I said. And they're all about girls. You know there's other things in life besides girls but they are the best and the worst things in a man's life. Besides what he told me, in time I found to be true myself.

A woman is a woman no matter the color, no matter the race. Women will stick together if it benefit them. An ugly woman needs love just like a pretty woman and may get it a lot quicker than a pretty woman. Fat or thin, love them equally. We men always had and will always have a love-hate relationship with women. One minute you love them the next you want to strangle them. A woman will make you want to walk on water when you know damn well you can't, but you try anyway. All these things I found out for myself and now I'm telling you. Well, thanks old man, I'll remember that. You do that young man, and pass it on.

Like I said, you meet all kinds of people in the park and they all have a story to tell, just watch and let your imagination do the rest. Sometimes when I'm walking and I see those individual driving and on their cell phones, I wonder what they have to say that can't wait until they get home or wherever they're going. The one that's really gets me is the wife that calls her husband at work just to say "hi honey "what you doing? And the husband would say "I'm at work, what you need? Oh, she said yes I just wanted to call and see how you doing. Meanwhile her speed has dropped from 50 to 35, Cars backed up behind her for half a mile and she's over in the left hand lane. Other cars started passing her on the right and she looks over at them and calls them an idiot.

It's not all bad being old believe it or not there is romance, dare I say more than I care to admit. The retirement center I live in has everything an old man needs. Three meals a day, pool and rec room. Relaxation room where you can intermingle and enjoy the other guest. Your medical staff, your apartment consist of one bedroom, some have two. A living room with a couch, lounge chair and table plus guest and big screen TV. Bathroom and kitchenette with washer and dryer. All the comforts of home without the upkeep, a Miniature apartment you could say.

One third of the complex is men and the other two thirds women, so you know! Everyone in the community was of retirement age, say 65+. And a lot of these seniors looking for love and a lot of them finding it. A few of them only looking for sex, and also finding it. I went to a wedding here at the center the other week and I must say we old folks were getting down. The 2 that got hitched were 76 and 82 respectfully. We must have partied close to 12:30 AM. I woke up the next morning with one of the bridesmaids in bed beside me. You would think life would get less complicated when you're older especially with the ladies, but I have to tell you it don't, Maybe more so.

Once my bridesmaid left out another knocked on my door to ask me to lunch, and invite me to go see the movie that was playing at the centers theater, Casablanca! I know you seen it she said but it's always worth seeing again. The next day Mrs. Mabel, A 68 year old retired English teacher call me and asked me if I wanted to take a walk in the garden after dinner and maybe go back up to her apartment for Cocktails. I didn't have any plans so I agreed, I walked over to my dresser drawer and check my supply of Viagra and said, yeah I think I'm ready. Since I've been watching Miss Mabel for a while now, this may be a three Viagra night.

Who says seniors don't have sexual desires, must be the younger generations that said it because we have just as much or as little as the young. When the young man gets in bed with his girl and can't perform has he ever wondered where it went, why can't he get it up? This never happened before. Well, it may have come over to us old dudes, we just borrowing it for a minute. Give it right back that is if you were wondering. And maybe the reason the young feel the way they do is that all the seniors are somebody's grandmother, grandfathers and they wouldn't do nothing like that.

I could never see my mother do that they say. Damn that! We have and we do so get over it.

After Miss Mabel and I walked into her apartment she started taking off her clothes and said why don't we forgo the cocktails, have you taken your little blue pills yet? The things that the seniors have that the youngsters don't, we don't have to BS each other, and we don't have that much time. We know what we won't before we step out and we go right to it. If you been around and it's assumed I have you would have taken your pills before your walk in the garden, that's my part.

ONCE THE CLOTHS were off and partway to the bedroom I notice the bed covers were turned down and cocktails were on both sides of the bed "seniors don't mess around "I'm wondering then would the three pills be enough. Sometime later I was laying back sipping my cocktail and I said "WOW' Mrs. Mabel, I'm sure glad I had my physical. Call me Gladys she said. And I'm not finish with you yet. Ditto Gladys! You could say I'm getting more sex now than when I was in my twenties, but with more sex there comes more complications. I have to learn to just say no, you would think as old as the ladies are they wouldn't get jealous but that would be a wrong assumption because they do and quite often. And if you don't watch yourself they'll fight over you. If you can imagine 70 and 80 year old seniors going to blows over you. In your teens and twenties you would laugh about those things but today it's just pathetic. So it's always wise to have some kind of a plan. I get up in the morning and have my breakfast, walked down to the park and walk around. After a couple of hours of that I'll go to lunch (not at the center) maybe at a neighborhood diner I found. Maybe go down to the local library, play some chess with a few old-timers I befriended underneath an old oak tree.

Dinnertime I'm back at the center and the calls begin. My phone only comes on after 7 and I've had those to say why I have it set up that way and why don't I own a cell phone. I tell them at my age why I need a cell phone, too easy to find me and who wants to be found. I'm never home between 9 AM and 5 so why my phone should be ringing off the hook and I'm not there. I get enough action after 7 with the phone calls and the knocks on the door, not to mention the notes underneath the door. Once the word is out that you are laying a little Pike they come from all around. Like I said I'm glad I'm in good shape.

4

Party time

One thing about seniors, 11 o'clock most of us are in the bed, sometimes with someone. For me I pace myself, Monday's, Wednesday's and Thursday no sex, a person has to know their limits. The ladies will wear you out if you let them, I had to damn wright lie a few times "I ran out of Viagra "I would say. Next shipment won't be in till the 1st of the month. One of the ladies fooled me once and told me not to worry, she just picked up a batch at the local Walgreens.

When you think you know most everything here it comes, a woman that slips it to you again, never fails. The ladies will take you through some changes but they show can make you feel good about it when there doing it. I use to have an old buddy who used to say, yeah, she did fuck over me but she show smelled good while doing it. For some men it's the women's Smell that does it, once they put that on you, plus the sex, you gonna holler uncle.

In the homes they also have their dramas, the latest happen right down the hall from me. He was on his deathbed and about to die. The three girlfriends were in the apartment, then his kids from one of the marriages was there and another two or three kids showed up, everybody looking for their share. On top of that they found four wills, each one given the next everything. And to piss everyone off royally he dated each one for the same day and time. I guess that was his way of saying, fuck um all. The wills will be in court for years the only ones that got away with anything was the ladies there in the center. He was buying them a little bit of everything, all the time. Diamonds mostly, you know our ladies have to have their diamonds.

I hear he was somewhat of a jokester, I guess he's proven that. By the time they went through his finances he had a total of $10, $1 for each of his relatives. The relatives tried to get the diamonds return from the ladies but since then two have died and passed their shear own to their grandkids and the other took hers to the pawnshop and divided the money between her grandkids. The center had plenty dramas like that, I've learned if you gonna give someone something, give it to them while you're alive.

Up on the 5th floor a husband was visiting his wife who had been in a coma for over 6 months. He had been coming twice a week religiously, bringing flowers and candy (the nurses ate the candy) and after a few days the flowers went bad, but he brought them right on. His wife and he were the only ones left in their family, they had no kids or friends and he was staying in his home alone. There was nothing he really did accept watch TV and feed the cat who was having a lot of problems of his own, and would have to be put down soon. On this day he got dressed in his best suit, shirt and favorite tie that he knew his wife loved. Put an extra shine on his shoes and socks that matched. Set down at the table and finished his coffee sipping the rest out of a saucer. It was a little over a mile to the center and he walk as usual taking his time and it was a beautiful day to do it. Normally he stopped at the gift shop and pick up flowers for his wife and a box of candy but today halfway to the center he spotted an older lady of about his age between (68 and 72) had misstep off the curve of the corner street and twisted her ankle. He stopped to help, asked her if she needed a medic and she said no just let me rest for a few minutes. He suggested they go over to a café that was nearby for a cup of tea and maybe her ankle would feel better after that. He helped her to the café and they took a booth and began to talk.

He asked her did she live around there and for how long. About 20 years she said and he told her he's been living around their about the same, except she lived in one direction and he the other. Funny they've never ran into one another he said. She said she was a widower of 5 years, no family or friends to speak up, she just watched TV and maybe go to the movies, to the library or park. I live a very quiet life, really. You Kind of wonder what's it's all about she said. Sometimes I feel like just ending it all. Do you know what I'm saying? I think I do he says and he went on to tell her his situation, no relatives or friends, lifestyle similar to hers. You know he said this is nice, sitting here talking to you, I haven't done this in a while. I could get used to this. You know she said I was thinking the same thing. There is a play Friday evening that I've been wanting to see, would you care to join me? I sure would, should I pick you up? That'll be fine, say 7 o'clock she said. He went on to the center after that, purchased his flowers and candy. Up to the floor his wife was on and checked in at the nurse's station. They informed him that there was no change in his wife's condition and soon he will have to make a decision on whether or not to remove life supports. After returning home he started removing his cloths but first he went to his closet and took down his old shoebox and return the 22 automatic he had taken out that morning.

ALL STORYS DIDN'T end like that, a few weeks before a lady came to see her husband dressed exquisitely, for a lady of 92 her husband had been in a coma for over three years. They had been married over 72 years. Twice a week she was there seeing him, this day the way she was dressed all of the nurses commented on how she looked. She smiled and spoke to everyone which she normally didn't do. Took the elevator to her husband's floor, took the box of candy and book to his room and put the candy on the dresser beside his bed. Kissed him on his forehead, sat down and started reading at the spot she had marked. 45 minutes later she put the book down walked over to her husband's bed kissed him on his forehead again, took the pistol out of her purse and shot him one time in the head. Put the pistol up to her own head and fired. When they found the two of them she was laying over him holding his hand.

Whenever I do go to lunch at the center there is always at least one lady at the table with me, most times two and sometimes three. Everyone jockeying for position. Now that's a hell of a site, all the women cutting each other down. They're not younger women, get to the point of wanting to fight but more settle. Like individuals playing chest or something, all trying to get a piece of the action "me". Now I know how it felt when there was four and five men around one woman. Felt like you're being pulled in all directions. Don't get me wrong it's not all bad and I'm not the only one but since the women outnumber us men two to one, it bee's like that. There are those men that kind of stay clear of the women for one reason or another and that means the rest of us has to pick up the slack, which some of us are willing to do.

But we all have our outlet, mine is going to the park three to four days a week and listen to my jazz music. I noticed another senior coming out the movies alone a few times a week, I guess that's his out. And on and on. But there was one old boy that would leave the center and meet up with another senior lady in the park, now he's just a hoe. Can't get enough I guess. Seniors get too much sex, maybe that's why we live as long as we do. Good sex, a glass of wine and a walk in the park. The best things in life are free, that's what the old people used to say.

5

AFTER THURSDAY

Thursday's in the park seems to be a good day, not very many people out the day just before Friday and everyone knows what Friday is, party time! Friday and Saturday, Sunday is supposed to be a day of rest except for the hard-core party players, they take it right back into Monday's. Hangovers, don't know where the week end went, saying they'll never do it again. A few waking up in bed with a woman they never saw before and will probably never see again. I guess that is better than ending up in Vegas married, like I heard one couple did. They hurried up and got an annulment. Yes, those were the days, you can have em!

On this day it was pretty quiet, about the way you would want a park to be. Not too many kids, everything moving at a slow pace. But then if you're observant and looking between the lines you'll still notice things.

Unit 15! This is dispatch! Go ahead dispatch, this is unit 15. Allied bank has just been robbed by two Hispanic males, between the ages of nineteen and twenty two. 5 foot 8 and 5'10, hundred and sixty-two and one hundred seventy pounds respectively. Blue Jeans, white shirts and Houston Astro baseball caps, White sneakers. There headed your way, hold your location.

Roger dispatch! Ofc. Philippe Rodriguez, age 23, stops in the park every morning at 10:15 in the same location for approximately 15 minutes. He had only recently gotten married and back off his honeymoon. He had been with the police department for two years and was planning to make it a career. He and his wife had looked at homes to purchase over the weekend and planning on having a family of no less than four kids. The future was all set up for them, life for him has gone as planned. Graduated high school, the first in his family. A year at a community college. Police Academy, and then married. Yeah, everything was going as planned.

You see anybody following us the driver said to his passenger? Yeah, we got at least one cop on our ass and you can bet there are others behind him. You think you'll be able to lose them? We'll give it one hell of a try the driver said. How much do you think we scored, the driver said? Well we hit them right at their transfer time, but we hit them big. What about the Dye pack the driver said? They had no chance to put it in, Is this as fast as this heap can go, you should have let me drive. Don't worry about it, I'm about to lose these pigs in just one minute. There is a park a little ways up that I use to go and there's a back way out, we'll be back in the hood before you know it.

Unit 15, this is dispatch come in! This is unit 15, go ahead dispatch. The two individual robbers of the Allied Bank has just turned off to the park but the trees are so thick that the helicopter may lose sight of them, so be on your toes. Roger dispatch. Hey, what are you doing, you're getting off the main roadway to the park. Yeah, I know said the driver. That cutoff I was telling you about starts here, this trail is large enough for our car and we only have to go through a small part of the park. We'll come out on the other side, call it a short cut. We just have to cross the parks baseball diamond. I can't see a damn thing, you sure you know where you're going? These trails never change, I can find my way blindfolded. Where you think I bought all my little honeys to. Don't you think you should slow down, you're going pretty fast and I can't see a damn thing in this Bush? Just look down at the trail, you can't get lost and I can't slow down, you forgetting the cops are chasing us. Hey I see on opening ahead, I told you I'd get us through this. Maybe you can slow this damn thing down now... Hey, hey watch out, watch out! Before they knew it they had ran into the back of Officer Rodriguez and his squad car. The driver's air bag deployed and knocked him out cold, broke his nose, knocked out his front teeth and put one of his eyes out. The passenger ended up being thrown through the windshield and on to the hood, breaking his leg, head fracture and crack ribs.

Rodriguez air bag deployed and broke his nose and knocked him out, part of the devise and hardware ended up in his head. Both vehicles were smoking and about to explode, three men were not in the best of shape. There was one old man in the area sitting on a bench, watching it all. He ran(more like walked) over to the damage automobiles, pulled the policeman out and attempted to pull the others away from theirs but got winded and couldn't do it. An explosion occurred in the vehicle and a red dye like substance bellowed out. By this time the other police units arrived and dragged the other two men out to safety. The old man was called a hero for saving the police officer and there is talk of giving him a citation. Thursday's in the park seems to be a good day, not very many people out the day just before Friday and everyone knows what Friday is, party time! Friday and Saturday, Sunday is supposed to be a day of rest except for the hard-core party players, they take it right back into Monday's. Hangovers, don't know where the week end went, saying they'll never do it again. A few waking up in bed with a woman they never saw before and will probably never see again. I guess that is better than ending up in Vegas married, like I heard one couple did. They hurried up and got an annulment. Yes, those were the days, you can have em!

On this day it was pretty quiet, about the way you would want a park to be. Not too many kids, everything moving at a slow pace. But then if you're observant and looking between the lines you'll still notice things.

Unit 15! This is dispatch! Go ahead dispatch, this is unit 15. Allied bank has just been robbed by two Hispanic males, between the ages of nineteen and twenty two. 5 foot 8 and 5'10, hundred and sixty-two and one hundred seventy pounds respectively. Blue Jeans, white shirts and Houston Astro baseball caps, White sneakers. There headed your way, hold your location.

 Roger dispatch! Ofc. Philippe Rodriguez, age 23, stops in the park every morning at 10:15 in the same location for approximately 15 minutes. He had only recently gotten married and back off his honeymoon. He had been with the police department for two years and was planning to make it a career. He and his wife had looked at homes to purchase over the weekend and planning on having a family of no less than four kids. The future was all set up for them, life for him has gone as planned. Graduated high school, the first in his family. A year at a community college. Police Academy, and then married. Yeah, everything was going as planned.

You see anybody following us the driver said to his passenger? Yeah, we got at least one cop on our ass and you can bet there are others behind him. You think you'll be able to lose them? We'll give it one hell of a try the driver said. How much do you think we scored, the driver said? Well we hit them right at their transfer time, but we hit them big. What about the Dye pack the driver said? They had no chance to put it in, Is this as fast as this heap can go, you should have let me drive. Don't worry about it, I'm about to lose these pigs in just one minute. There is a park a little ways up that I use to go and there's a back way out, we'll be back in the hood before you know it.

Unit 15, this is dispatch come in! This is unit 15, go ahead dispatch. The two individual robbers of the Allied Bank has just turned off to the park but the trees are so thick that the helicopter may lose sight of them, so be on your toes. Roger dispatch. Hey, what are you doing, you're getting off the main roadway to the park. Yeah, I know said the driver. That cutoff I was telling you about starts here, this trail is large enough for our car and we only have to go through a small part of the park. We'll come out on the other side, call it a short cut. We just have to cross the parks baseball diamond. I can't see a damn thing, you sure you know where you're going? These trails never change, I can find my way blindfolded. Where you think

I bought all my little honeys to. Don't you think you should slow down, you're going pretty fast and I can't see a damn thing in this Bush? Just look down at the trail, you can't get lost and I can't slow down, you forgetting the cops are chasing us. Hey I see on opening ahead, I told you I'd get us through this. Maybe you can slow this damn thing down now... Hey, hey watch out, watch out! Before they knew it they had ran into the back of Officer Rodriguez and his squad car. The driver's air bag deployed and knocked him out cold, broke his nose, knocked out his front teeth and put one of his eyes out. The passenger ended up being thrown through the windshield and on to the hood, breaking his leg, head fracture and crack ribs.

Rodriguez air bag deployed and broke his nose and knocked him out, part of the devise and hardware ended up in his head. Both vehicles were smoking and about to explode, three men were not in the best of shape. There was one old man in the area sitting on a bench, watching it all. He ran(more like walked) over to the damage automobiles, pulled the policeman out and attempted to pull the others away from theirs but got winded and couldn't do it. An explosion occurred in the vehicle and a red dye like substance bellowed out. By this time the other police units arrived and dragged the other two men out to safety. The old man was called a hero for saving the police officer and there is talk of giving him a citation.

Now what am I going to do with a citation at my age?

Breaking news... Senior saves life of police officer at the local park, only to have the officer die on the way to the hospital!

IF YOU LIVE long enough you'll see and hear things you thought was passé but eventually come back. Back on my usual bench one morning, not too long after the robbery incident there was another senior walking a young kid of about 5 years old holding her hand. Earlier there was on Amber alert of a small child being abducted. The only reason I mention this is that the old man was black and the little girl was white. The policemen who was touring The area stop their squad car and approach the older gentleman, snatched his hand from the little girls and asked him what was he doing with that little white girl, she must be the one that had been abducted. By the way the officer was acting, manhandling the old man the little girl started crying. That's okay little girl, the mean old man won't hurt you anymore the police officer said while putting cuffs on the senior. You're the mean one the little girl said, and you leave my pa pa alone.

Breaking news... Police harassing senior citizen for walking his granddaughter in the park.

If you get to be 101 its best you never assume anything!

The senior center is set up like a small town, the same old people just a little older. Thief's, scams and frauds, they're all there. There are those that use the ladies for more than sex and vice versa, they will also rip them off. I try to school them in my own little way but a woman wants what she wants. The crazy thing is the thief steal from the ladies to give to another lady. The ladies steal from the men to buy diamonds so the men can steal from them to give to other women. Crazy! It's like a merry-go-round, one time up and one time down.

One thing I've noticed, when you give a woman a diamond, they never asked where it came from, all they see is the diamond. I only gave out one diamond in my life and that was to my wife when we first got married. The price of a diamond at that time was so cheap even I could afford one.

I've been given diamonds, a number of times, by ladies. Some would always tell me, this was my dead's husbands and I'd like you to have it, bullshit! I never believed that for one minute, but I'm no fool, I took it as it was given to me. And in turn sometimes I would play the same game, give a lady something and say it was my mother's and I wanted her to have it (games). We never tire of playing them even the seniors. I even had a little trinket box that I used to give out little doodads now and then, I'd get it from one and give to the other.

A couple of pieces I even took down to the pawn shop to have it appraised, all cheap stuff so that's what I give back, it's only fair.

Another day, another walk in the park. I wonder what I can expect today. Kids at play, young lovers wondering and looking forward to the future, maybe a little crime. A senior citizen sees all those things, how else would we make it through the day.

."

CENTRALE

This novel is a continuation of a short story taken from Ducks in a Row... Fictional lockup.

John Chandler and the alien, Centrale.

Lockup 6x9... part 2

JOHN! JOHN! Are you there, John?

Is that you Centrale? How in the hell did you ever reach me? I thought you couldn't call me and when did you get back?

Things change John, Just like your technology. Did you ever get out of prison?

Well, yes and no. I was out for a minute and then my feelings got the best of me and I lost it.

So you're in the same spot I left you 18 months ago, Centrale said. Pretty much, John said.

How long have you got this time?

Oh, about 13 more months, if things go according to plans. But then as you know I said that the last time. You know I didn't know how hard it would be without your help, these 18 months have been more like 18 years. Is there no way you can get me out of here so I won't have to come back?

I'm afraid not John, but I can continue the arrangement we had before. That should make life a little easier for you while you're there. How is your girlfriend John, Irma was it? And how did she feel about the extra time you doing?

She didn't take it to good and I haven't heard or seen her in the past eighteen months, since she drove away from the front gate.

I could send you to her apartment if she was still there but I'm afraid she's not, Centrale said.

But you could find her if you wanted to John said.

Yes I could Centrale said but I think it would be better all-around if you let her be, after all you wasn't that crazy about her anyway. If you had left with me on that trip, you were going to leave her anyway.

Now, how did you know that John said?

I know lots of things John and I have gotten to know you pretty well over time, Centrale said.

Okay John said. You're not going to transport me to Irma's, you're not going to get me out of here permanently so what are you willing to do? Not that I'm complaining mine you, I still have thirteen months to go.

Yes you do John, and since you do maybe you can do something for me. Something that I am unable to do for myself.

Damn Centrale, I thought you could do everything, on this earth and beyond. You got the power!

Oh, I can't do everything John, that's why I'm gonna need you.

You need me, and all this time I've been needing you. Well Centrale how in the world could I be of service to you? If you remember I only have six to seven hours freedom per night.

I know that John and I have a solution, leave it to me.

What is it you won't me to do? John asked.

You do understand John, if there was anyone else I could turn to I would, but since I don't and this has to be taken care of I chose you. Someone I can trust and dare I say, you owe me. Yeah, yeah Centrale, I'm aware of that what do you won't me to do?

A few years ago I met Centrale in a park after a little spat with Irma in which she called the police and I hightailed it before they got there, In the park I met an alien from a distant planet(Centrale), for some reason he toke a liken to me and I was in awe of him.

Before he left he gave me a way to contact him but since I was drinking at the time I chalked it all up as the alcohol and a bad dream.

It was close to a year and a half and 6 months in the hole before I figured it out.

I contacted Centrale and he started giving me things that you couldn't otherwise get in the hole.

Like good food, books and TV, transported me to my woman's apartment and other places in the world. It was so nice that when it came time to leave I didn't want to go. So I raised enough hell that they gave me more time on top of the time I had. I end up spending close to three years in their before they turn me loose. At the gate on my last day with Irma waiting for me I did a stupid thing, I hit one of the guards that had been harassing me for all that time and before I could get out the gate and to Irma, they put me back in the hole for additional eighteen months. I never heard from Irma again and Centrale had left for another galaxy. Now after no contact with Centrale, and it was hard, here he show up again, Well better late than never. Before we do anything I said I'm gonna need me some decent food and some drawls.

I think I can handle that, Centrale said.

LOMPOC, CALIFORNIA, summer 2009…A small little town that grown immensely over the years where you would love to bring up your kids. Five or six small parks access to the beach, never heard of an air-conditioner, in the evening everyone needed a light jacket. Very little crime maybe because there was one of the largest prisons in the country right outside town. It would have stayed that way if it hadn't been for an incident that happened, and all hell broke loose.

Johnny Atkins, a hard working citizen with a wife and two small kids, a job with the local phone company, large mortgage and a six and eight year old Toyotas. One paid off and one still with nine months to go.

All and all he was doing pretty well, until. A policeman was chasing a speeder that had a back light out and wouldn't stop when he was ordered to and the chase began. It went thru the main street of town to the residential section, the kid was in the street when the speedster turned the corner to where she was. He managed to avoid her but the policeman didn't, he ended up knocking the kid 50 feet into Johnny's neighbor's driveway. After stopping for a second and not getting out of the car the officer continued his pursuit after his suspect.

Johnny ran over to his daughter and held her in his arms and cried. Someone call 911 and his daughter was taken to the local hospital where she was pronounced dead on arrival. When the policeman was confronted to why he didn't stop and render aid, he had no explanation. Just that he had to catch the suspect who was eventually captured and was convicted of evading arrest and a broken tail light.

The police officer was put on suspension and desk duty for further investigation. Johnny felt he should have been fired immediately. After two months nothing had been done, his daughter had been buried, the officer was back on the job them saying something about he was only doing his job and accidents will happen.

7

EYE FOR AN EYE

Johnny started drinking and lost his job also lost one of his cars and got behind on his mortgage. His wife couldn't deal with the changes in him so she left with their remaining son and went to her mother's in another state. After six months Johnny didn't look like the same man. Hadn't shaved in weeks, his hygiene was to be desired, looked like he slept in his cloths for weeks. That's when he decided to kill the police officer that murdered his daughter and did this to him. Johnny went down to the basement and found his old 45 he had hidden locked in his old army trunk, check the clip and fondled it in his hands, feels just like yesterday, I guess you never lose that loving feeling. He thought his killing days were over after Vietnam, just one more he thought, just one more. He found the policeman after six hours of searching at a fast food establishment, he parked right beside his squad car and waited when he walked out and got within a few feet of his car Johnny got out of his car, walked up to him with his 45 out. When the officer saw him his eyes went wide, he knew him and why he was there but nothing he could do." Tell my daughter I love her "then Johnny shot the officer between the eyes set down and waited for the authorities. In the interview room they asked him why he shot the officer and he said because he killed my daughter. That was ruled on accident one of the interviewers said, he was exonerated. Not in my eyes Johnny said. You've taken my daughter, my wife left me taking my other child, I'm about to lose my house and I've turned into an alcoholic. You've taken everything from me so now I took one of yours. Yes you did Mr. Atkins and now you're going to pay for it, maybe with your life. Everyone's talking about the officer and his family, no one said a word about me and mine. Society is playing me as the bad guy, I hear not a word about my daughter. I think officer if society don't give a damn about me and my family then I won't give a damn about them. Therefore I'll give society and the city of Lompoc an ultimatum. Set me free! Set me free now and I'll forgive but not forget what you've done to me and my family. The officer looked at Johnny in astonishment, are you threatening this department and society as a whole Mr. Atkins? You know that's really laughable. If this wasn't such a serious matter I would have to laugh but you are here accused of the murder of a police officer and you won't be getting out no time soon.

AFTER SEEING THE judge and him setting his bond at two million dollars, the judge asked Johnny was there anything he wanted to say. Yes judge there is, set me free, now. The judge looked at him in disbelief and said, I'm afraid I can't do that and it looks like you'll be incarcerated for a long time. So be it judge but the next time we meet you'll be begging to let me go. Guard, will you take this fool away, the judge said. The reporters in the courtroom reported the conversation between the judge and Johnny and ran it on the local news and TV. From there it went nationally.

Murderer defies judge, says Set me free! The national news wanted to know more about the killer of a police officer who admitted it and demands to be set free. CNN got an interview with Johnny and he told them the story of his little girl being hit by the police car, they not stopping. The policeman being let off and the city not offering on apology. He felt it was an eye for an eye.

I understand your grief and I'm sorry for your loss but you do understand that they're not going to ever let you go the reporter said. Our system of justice just don't work that way. And really, what are you going to do if they don't release you, breakout?

No, Johnny said. They will let me out, not only that they will beg me to leave. You will have to explain that one to me the news person said.

In two weeks it will come in three stages, the life as we know it now will cease for a While, say a week at first then longer. What is 'it' the news person said?

Let's start with cell phones, the item that society is so crazy about right now. What they can't seem to do without. The gadget they can't walk down the street without having it up to their ear, can't take care of business at the bank or convenience store without that damn phone to their ear. Can't drive their automobiles, walk in the park or at the beach. Yes, I think I'll start with that first.

You know the newsperson said, all this sounds kind of far-fetched, when is all this supposed to happen? If I'm not released in two weeks then, say on a Monday. And how long will this blackout last? Two weeks then we'll go on to the second phase. And what will the second phase be the news person asked? I'll tell you that after the first phase start, I know you'll be back. You know if you could do that you'll hurt a lot of people, did you ever consider that? Did society ever think about hurting me and mine? Besides, you ever heard of a Rotary phone Johnny asked.

So you see John we have a problem! Why is it that 'we' have a problem, why can't you just stop him? And by the way how in the hell did he get such power in the first place? John you wasn't the first human we reached out to, there were others. This one we gave powers to and before we left thought we wiped his mind clean of everything we gave him, but it seems like we didn't and now we can't take it back. If you can't do anything how can I help? It's like this John, it's true we can't do anything where we are but you being on earth and a human can. And how's that Centrale? By certain powers we are prepared to give you. Has this guy we're talking about have the same powers John said? His name is Johnny Atkins and yes he do. What kinds of powers are we talking about John asked?

JAMISON!

   YEAH, CHIEF?

How did you make out with that Atkin's fellow? Did you find out anything we didn't already know? You could say that but you may not want to print it. Well tell me what you got and I'll decide that, shoot. Okay, he's threatening the authorities to let him out or he's going to do something bad to the city, then he won't be so hard on them. How's that, you're joking right, say you're joking. No chief I'm not joking that's what he said. The guard was right there in the room with me when he said it. We can't print no crazy shit like that they'll laugh us out of town. We've been waiting for your byline and we have nothing else to go in that spot so I guess we'll have to go with you, but just clean it up some. Maybe he's trying to get away with being crazy when he shot the cop Jamison said. What's he talking about going to piss everyone off, the chief said? Cutting everyone's cell phone off Jamison said. That'll do it, the chief said. If anything it would take to piss off society it's cutting off their damn cell phones. Have it on my desk in an hour. By the way the chief said, when did he say all this was supposed to take place? Two weeks, Jamison said.

I'll tell you what, write two articles, the safe one and the outrageous one. Better safe than sorry! After reading Jamison's articles the chief decided to go with the most outrageous one. His thinking was that maybe the paper could milk it for the next two weeks. Like a countdown. Day 14 Day 13 to Day 12. On down to the day of the suppose shut down of the phone, knowing all the time that nothing like that could ever happen.

What kind of powers are we talking about Centrale?

 1st Centrale said you'll be able to transport yourself anywhere you like in the world without my help,

2nd you want ever have to worry about getting attacked or shot or anything like that.

If you were then whoever were to try then it would backfire on them. If you were incarcerated like you are now the authorities couldn't hold you, you could just slimly walk out.

If that's the case John said, then why wouldn't this Atkins guy just walk out? Because John Mr. Atkins want this to happen, he wants his revenge no matter what he tells the people. He wants to bring havoc on the ones that did this to him and his family. Well if he can get out anytime he wants why wouldn't I after you give me this power? Because John, we still have that hold on you where we don't on Mr. Atkins. We will cover for you as long as you're doing this job for us and then will bring you back to continue your sentence. Don't worry John, it won't be all that bad.

You never did tell me how you were going to cover for me? John said. We'll just put in a double for you, no one will ever know, trust me! And how do I stop Atkins from doing the things he says he's going to do? And how far do I go. That's up to you John, I'm sure you'll come up with something. There is one other thing Centrale said. You won't be able to do anything until he starts acting on what he says he's going to do. In the meantime what am I supposed to do, John said. You said you wanted to get out of there, and get some decent food and get you some (drawls) as you put it.

Your time will be well taken care of until you meet Mr. Atkins. Sit back, relax and enjoy yourself.

DAY 7 AND Jamison wrote… A week has gone by and that day is coming where we all will lose cell phone service and will need rotary phones, says Mr. Atkins. Are you shaken in your boots yet? I don't know what I'll do when that happens, if that happens. My whole life's in that damn phone and I'll be up the creek, literally. I know you all have thought about it even though we know it'll never happen, could it? Day 10 CNBC came to the jail to visit Atkins and they asked him about his prediction? What about it Johnny said. This could never happen right, you are just putting everyone on. I said what I said and my prediction will come true if I'm not release from this jail. 4 days and counting, tell your government to set me free. Mr. Atkins it's your government to, you don't expect them to cut you lose after you kill one of their police officers. There, you just said it. There police officers not mine. He used to be mine but then he went and kill my kid. But we've been all over this before, I don't see there being anything else to talk about. In 4 days all hell is going to break loose, the cell phone lovers are going to pitch a bitch. Besides the police officer who else are you blaming for your daughter's death? I'm blaming everyone, society in general because they had the chance to speak out and they didn't. 1st phase is about to convene and the only way you can stop it is to set me free. Now that's all I'm saying, guard I'm ready to go back to my cell now. The last day of the prediction Jamison wrote her last article…Well this is it, the day before Johnny Atkins prediction comes true or not. Which way are you leaning? If the phones do go out in the city, I don't even want to think about it. At noon tomorrow we'll all know and either let Mr. Atkins out of jail or call him a big fat fraud. Regardless I think Mr. Atkins has everyone's attention as of now. I like to get your opinion on what's happening the last two weeks and how it's affected you one way or another has it been affecting you, will it affect you if it happens, do you care? Who would you blame if it does happen? Johnny Atkins, the police or society itself. We'll find out tomorrow, call me!

The final day, 10:30 AM…

There's something about the town that is unsettling, the people don't seem to be acting the same, walking the same or driving the same.

Few people seem to be talking on their cell phones, just checking to see if it was still on. The younger folks saying it's just a bunch of B.S, no one can cut off cell phones it'll take the government to do something like that, besides the cell phones were off the satellites and that's miles into space. No one man can do all that. The seniors were thinking just the opposite, they remember the depression and wasn't taking any chances. A lot of them still remember the old rotary phones and felt they could really do without any phones, after all during their time very few had phones anyway.

They also knew about being prepared, a lot of them still had windup clocks. As the time wind down to the noon hour more and more people were worrying what would happen and how long would it lasts if it did. Would they release Johnny Atkins if it did happen? Others were saying, even if it did happen the authorities would never let him go, it would be a cold day in hell before that happens. At the 11 AM hour people started wondering just how many things are dependent on the cell phones, starting with just talking to somebody(of course very little of that's done anymore) kids talking to who knows who. Texting, which a lot of that's done. GPS, that'll be out. Google, playing games, that's out the only good thing is that they'll probably have less accidents. Less people walking into phone poles or walking into swimming pools, or each other. So I'm sure something good will come out of this.

8

ALL HELL

11:45 AM and the world is waiting to see what's going to happen to the small town of Lompoc, California. And wondering if something do happen will it affect them and how bad. And no one has mentioned the 2nd and 3rd phase that Atkins spoke of, what will those be?

 12 noon and nothing happened, the phones were on as usual, the apps were there, the games were there and Google was also there, everyone breathed a sigh of relief. Whether they wanted to admit it or not. Comments were, I knew it was a bunch of B.S from the start. People were texting their mothers, sisters, brothers and friends. Saying I told you so, now we all know that sucker is crazy. Now we can write him off and hang him for killing that cop, we shouldn't even give him a trial.

TWO MINUTES LATER into one person's text their phone went dead. All over town their cell phones went dead. The police and their constituents, the fire department, the water and electric district. The library and all that use a cell phone, the only phones that were in use in the city were land lines. Most people had given them up for cell phones and now what they were used to just two minutes ago, they no longer have. They didn't want to believe Atkins prediction. Some people were knocking their phones up against the wall trying to get them to come on. The cell phone company were inundated with people in their stores wanting to know what was wrong with their phones. The stores were no help because their phones were dead to. The radios and TV's were still on and that's how everyone were getting there news.CNN reported: Cell phones off as predicted, what now? NBC Reported: Lompoc, CA. you've got a problem. CBS: Its clobbering time! Somebody's gonna pay for this. This reaction from the persons in the street; I feel the loss, I've never been without my cell phone before, one lady said. What I'm I going to do? Even though the phone were off people were still trying to turn them on. I can't call the hospital to cancel my appointments one said. I'll have to find a land line for that. The people in the street had to acknowledge each other because their heads were no longer looking down. People on the buses, riding bikes and walking in the park no longer were wearing ear buds, eventually everyone in town started convening on the jail and Johnny Atkins. Some were wanting him to be let go and others wanted him hung immediately. By day three the town was in a real panic, the mayor and city Council all wanted to see Johnny Atkins. Mr. Adkins, are you the cause of all this, the mayor said? What you think Mr. Mayor, Johnny said. And it's not like you didn't have time to prepare. You know there are people out there that's asked him that we hang you right now, are you aware of that? Are you aware of the consequences if that were to happen, your precious cell phones won't be operational for the next 50 years. The interview room was so crowded with the mayor city Council members, chief of police and the likes, there were hardly any room for the guards. The only seat that was guaranteed was for the mayor and Johnny. Mr. Atkins we don't know how you did it but if it's within your power we wish you would stop it, you're hurting a lot of people. The people Mr. Mayor hurt me, Atkins said. The only way I'll stop what's happening is for you to release me. Mr. Atkins you know we can't do that, society won't stand for it. You mean the same society that's out there begging for their cell phones? In the same society that wouldn't speak up when my daughter was murdered? I'm asking you to think about your fellow man. What else can we do besides letting you go? Nothing else will do Mr. Mayor, except that.

That night, the mayor and city councilpersons, chief of police were in a private meeting trying to figure out what to do about Atkins. With the city losing thousands of dollars and it's just days after the blackout of the cellphones. Tomorrow it will be thousands more and then it will get into the millions. The citizens are mad as hell, what do you think they'll be like in a day or two? Pretty soon they'll be rioting in the streets. My wife is starting to raise hell at me because she can't call her friends and I know everyone in this room is in the same predicament. And besides that the whole world is laughing at us. So what do we do?

An unknown voice rang out "let's kill him "the room got very quiet, who said that, the mayor said. Who said that? Whoever said it, another councilman said. Is that such a bad idea to think about? After all is there any doubt that we're going to execute him anyway? After he dies the blackout will be lifted. Well now, remember what he said, someone else said. If something happens to him then the blackout may continue for another 50 years. Do anyone really believe that, I don't! Said another. Maybe you don't another councilmember said, but the same was said about him doing what he did, I believe him. Okay the mayor said, let's take a vote on it.

After the vote with the yea winning by a large margin it was asked who would carry out the action. Chief, would you be willing to execute it? Dam right mayor, just give me the word!

You got it! The mayor said.

The chief suggested that they let Atkins out on bond, once out he would have one of his SWAT team snipers take him out as he leaves the courthouse.

Mr. Atkins the judge said, the powers that be have thought it best to release you above my objections but that's what they want. Two days with no cell phones and they're willing to let a cop killer go. Because killing a policeman and you costing the city thousands of dollars, you want get away with it and you'll be back.

I hear you judge, all you have to do is not sign those papers and send me back to my cell, I don't think you have the balls, Atkins said. Guard, get Mr. Atkins to hell out of my court. On the way out of the court house there were at least 100 reporters from all over the world. A news podium was set up waiting for him to speak and answer questions. One of the first questions he was asked was when will the cell phones be turned back on? 24 hours after I leave my cell, that is if nothing goes wrong, Atkin said. What do you mean by that a reporter asked?

First of all I do not believe a word the city of Lompoc says, plus they caved in too easily. Why do you think they did that, besides the cell phones and money they were losing? Another reporter asked. You have to ask the mayor and his people that, they'll lie to you but you can ask them. After the questioning and Atkins was leaving he was walking down the courthouse stairs and across the street, the tried story window an explosion blew the window out and part of the frame. Behind the window and frame a man in a black uniform followed hanging on to part of a rifle. All of the reporters ran over to where the man lay across the street and started taking pictures. All notice that he wore the uniform of the Lompoc city Police Department SWAT team. The individual reporters that were first on the scene ran to their vans to call their networks. Some of the cameramen had caught the action live, one anchorman was saying it had been an assassination attempt by what look like a LC PD SWAT member. As far as I could see look like he's dead the anchorman said. It won't be till an autopsy before anybody knows for sure. If the explosion didn't kill him, then the three-story fall did. Now you see what I'm talking about Atkins told one of the reporters, which makes it easier to do what I have to do.

JAMAICA

JOHN! JOHN! ARE you there John? Damn Centrale you show call a guy at the most an opportune times. John was in bed with a Jamaican beauty and getting down for the third time that night. He had only met her that afternoon on the beach.

You really like hurting me don't you Centrale, how about giving me the rest of the night to finish this? John you had over a week and now it's time to get serious. Next stop for you will be Lompoc, California and Mr. Johnny Atkins.

Holiday hotel in Lompoc, room 242, three days after the attack on Atkins and his release. John was sitting on the bed reading the local paper. The mood around this town haven't been good. Mr. Atkins delivered on what he said he was going to do and as predicted the city is losing money hand over fist. No one can reach us unless they call on a landline. A lot of people were using their business only on their cell phones, now they have to stay in their office. Now they can no longer ride around in their cars or walk to the cafeteria or bathroom with cells in their hands. This network even finds itself in a fix, so if you try to call us and the line is busy... The paper went on to say that the attempted assassination on Atkins was being investigated and the State Department was looking into his release. He may end up being re-arrested. Centrale had told John that the phone blackout will last only a week then it will go to another phase if Atkins elected to do so. A week John said, this town will really be on pins and needles by that time. These people are acting crazy now, hundreds of people are starting to congregate around the courthouse not to mention Atkins home. I think we may have a riot going on soon. What do you want to do Centrale?

What do you want to do John, after all that's what we sent you there for?

The only thing I can think of is to talk to him and ask his intentions and go from there.

That's up to you John but remember, the next phase will be stronger then the last, you're going to have to be prepared to do something.

The courthouse meeting room 8 PM secret session; the mayor and his staff, plus the chief of police. Chief! What happened? Damn if I know mayor, the last I heard from my man was that he was taking the shot and all hell broke loose. From the autopsy we learn that the rifle he was firing exploded, it was so powerful it blew the whole damn window out. How in the hell could that happen chief, you say his weapon blew up? Bottom line yes, said the chief. He was dead before he hit the ground. I'm not believing this said the mayor, it's got to be more to it. Besides that we got them damn FEDS nosing around, what we gonna tell them? I suggest we tell them we had a man just go berserk because Atkins kill a fellow officer, the chief said. That sounds reasonable. Okay let's go with that said the mayor. You know the feds are insisting that we rearrests Atkins, one of the councilmen said, what are we gonna do about that? Well they hold the ball, I guess that's what we'll have to do. The mayor said. I got a feeling this is not going to play out too well the chief said. When do you want to do this? Let's wait until tomorrow, that's when Atkins said the blackout would end, 24 hours after he was released. He lied, it's lasted almost a week now. Yeah, but that was before the assassination try, we don't know how long it's going to last now, another person said. At one o'clock tomorrow afternoon it should tell us, that'll be six days really and we'll go get him then. Well he's sure not hiding one said, he's right there at his home.

HEY, WHO THE hell are you and how did you get in here? Atkins said. My name is John Chandler and I believe we have a mutual friend. And who would that be Atkins said? His name is Centrale. Centrale! What do you know about Centrale? He asked me to stop by and see you. Do you happen to have a drink? Check the bar over in the corner, help yourself. How did you meet Centrale, Atkins asked? About the same way you did John said. So there were others beside myself Atkins said. Yes there were others, there are others. But Centrale sent you to see me as if I didn't know why Atkins said. He wants you to stop what you're doing, what you are about to do John said. Are you aware of what they did to my family, to me? I am John said and I sympathize with you but you are hurting a lot of people. Fuck the people, Atkins said. No one ever thought about me and mine.

At one o'clock that afternoon a knock came at Atkins door, John Chandler and Atkins were in the den. Atkins got up and open the door and the chief of police, two plain clothes officers and four uniforms were there. The press were there and a crowd of onlookers of about 300. Mr. Atkins the chief said. We're here to arrest you for the murder of Ofc. Mud Wilder. Atkins turned around and looked at

John and said. Sorry, I have to go. Outside the officers attempted to put handcuffs on him but they wouldn't lock. Then they tried slip cuffs but they wouldn't lock either. Then Atkins told them that he wouldn't be cuffed, one of the officers decided to get a little rough on Atkins and throw him up against the car and Atkins used his elbow to hit him in the stomach and the officers got perturbed and pull his stunned gun. The chief told the officer not to tease him but before he did the officer had fired. 50,000 votes left the gun but none hit Atkins, they all stayed with the officer given him the full 50,000 Volts. He fell to the ground twitching and convulsing. The other officers ran over to him trying to help. One of the other officers was so mad at what happened to his comrade that he pulled his stun gun and fired at Atkins and the same thing happened to him. Two of the other officers pulled their service revolvers and Atkins said. If you fire those weapons you will lose the hand that you fired from. Now, I'll agree to be arrested but I won't be handcuffed Atkins said. Then you are telling us you won't be arrested, one of the officers said. Whatever, Atkins said.

Chief! Everyone looked toward the chief for instructions, whatever way we can get him back into a cell let's do it the chief said. Two detectives escorted Atkins to the rear of a police car, without cuffs. The stun gun officers were being treated by the medics. The newspaper people were catching everything on camera and within minutes it was all around the world. Four o'clock that afternoon

Atkins was in front of that same judge. I told you you'd be back, sooner than I thought but here you are. They'll be no bond set for you so be prepared to make yourself comfortable.

Judge, I elected to be taken into custody and I will leave whenever I damn well please, you remember that.

10

BRAKEING NEWS

Breaking news... Johnny Atkins was taken back into custody today but not without controversy and a scuffle. Two deputies were hurt with their own stun guns when they tried to fire on Atkins. Two other offices decided to pull their pistols when Atkins informed them that if they did and fire then they would lose their hand. I think they believed him, they didn't fire. No word still about our cell phones it's been going on for four days now and the city is going crazy. The world is laughing at us but I have to say that the 2nd phase will be coming up soon. We don't know what that will be. I predict cell phone blackouts for the rest of the world. From this reporter's viewpoint, I think we should take our losses and give Mr. Atkins what he wants.

Almost a week to the day and the town were at their wits in and the fighting in the streets had torn the city apart. But the kids were playing outside again, playgrounds were full. Neighbors talking to one another, there were no talking to neighbors when they were on their cell phones. The phones came back on, just like that. The scene was like the cities baseball team just won the pennant. But then the town went back the way it was before the phones were turned off. The friendships that were formed after the phones were turned off, went dead again once the phones came back on. Everything back to normal, for now.

2nd phase. Period. The day after the phones came back on. Atkins walked out of the city jail, he opened his cell door and walked down the corridor pass the holding cell. Then pass the booking area, picked up a bottle of water at the Sgt. Station. No one realized it until he was walking down the courthouse stairs, then twenty police officers came storming out the doors guns in hand. The media was still across the street some 25 of them with cameras rolling. The Sgt. that was in charge of the uniforms told Atkins to stop or he'd fire. Atkins kept right on walking. The Sgt. warn Atkins again to stop or he'd shoot, Atkins kept right on walking. Fifteen to twenty guns were all pointing at Atkins waiting on the Sgt. to fire or something. No one ever considered teasing him again. So the Sgt. repeated once more, stop or I'll shoot. Atkins kept right on walking.

The Sgt. and fifteen others fired, all fifteen pistols exploded in the offices hands, and all fifteen lost their hands. There was a few that was hesitant to fire and that was the only thing that saved their hand. Medics were call from all over the city to assist the offices.

 Atkins walked a block down the street to a Mac Donald's restaurant and purchased a big Mac, fries and a Coke.

JOHN WAS STILL sitting in the den in Atkins home watching everything on TV. Atkins walking down the courthouse stairs, the police telling him to stop and him ignoring them and they opened fire on him. There guns exploding and taking off their hands, all accept a few had injuries. Atkins was seen still walking down the street and out of sight. Within seconds all that happen went around the world and everyone was wondering," what's next"

Atkins has said he'd accept nothing less than an unconditional release. Some felt he didn't want a release, just to bring havoc on the town. Since the phones are back on everybody is looking toward phase two. What could that be?

What the hell is it going to take the mayor said to his councilmembers? The only thing I can think of is a pardon from the governor, and who ever heard of a pardon for a cop killer. Can anyone think of a way to get rid of this ass hole?

Let's try the SWAT team again in force this time, maybe we can overwhelm him.

What the hell can they do that the fifteen cops firing at him couldn't do? Plus we short one SWAT member, don't forget that.

What did the Feds say, the chief said? All they're saying is that there working on it, the mayor said. What I'd like to know is where did Atkins get all this power from, could he have had it all along? He was all right until one of your cops ran over his kid, all he asked for was for someone to acknowledge it. Maybe apologize but no, all we could tell the man was shit happens. One of the councilmembers said. I think I'd be a little mad to if that happened to me. Has anyone ever thought that Atkins is getting help from "up there "and pointed up. God! You mean God one of the consul person said? No, I don't mean God, I mean from outer space, we can't rule that out.

So now we talking about some damn aliens, we believing in aliens now? Fuck that. I believe if anything someone is screwing around with our satellites, the mayor said. That's a better scenario then the fed come up with anyway. Hey, said the chief. Maybe it's over, the cell phones are back on and everything seems to be back to normal.

I got a feeling it's not over until he gets what he wants, another said. How are your people in the hospital doing, the mayor asked the chief, they doing any better? If you call 15 policemen with their hands blown off doing any better than the answer is no.The department is losing people left and right, two dead, two in the hospital with Taser burn, 15 with their hands blown off. Oh yeah, we're doing fine. Keep on like this and we'll need a whole new department. What about locating his wife, maybe she can talk some sense into him. We already tried locating her and she's not responding, the chief said. Well, keep trying the mayor said. That's all we have left especially if phase two pop up.

John? Yes Centrale! Are you making any headway with Mr. Atkins? No I'm not, they picked him up before I had a chance to talk to him. And I guess you heard what happened next. Yes Centrale said, it's starting to get bad and you're waiting on what, Centrale said?

I expect him back at the house soon and I'll continue the conversation with him, I'll let you know how it goes.

John, Centrale said. Be careful!

WHEN JOHNNY HAD ordered his food the people in McDonald's had recognized him when he walked in, the manager told him," no charge " he went over to a window table and sit down and started eating his lunch, before long a few kids came over to him and asked if he was some kind of a superhero? Yeah, he said. Why don't we just say that I am? I'm here to get rid of all the lying scum bags out there. Are the police lying scumbags one said? Yeah, they are. They murdered my little girl! They said it was an accident we heard, one kid said. No matter Johnny said, they killed her anyway, and they'll pay. What about little kids like us? The only advice I can give you is just stay out the way, Johnny said. Now, get the hell away from me.

A customer that was in the establishment and overheard said to Johnny, that's no way to talk to young kids. A musclebound young man of about 20 said, I think you need to be taught a lesson. Johnny just looked at him and told him to go away. The customer kicked his chair out the way and headed toward him, when he reached within three feet Johnny put up his left hand, palm toward the young man and a beam of light hit him Square in the chest and knocked him back through the plate glass window and into the parking lot. Johnny got up and walked out passing the young man laid out on the parking lot grounds, he never moved.

I'll be got damn the chief said. If he hasn't done it again. If blowing off our officers hands wasn't enough he goes and throw a Mac Donald's customer through the window. They say he's paralyzed from the waist down. When is it going to stop? We need some kind of intervention and we need it now.

When Atkins walked through the door of his home, through a maze of reporters and only a few cops, FBI agents, state troopers and county police. But none of them tried to stop him. You still hear he said to John? I'm still here, we haven't finished our conversation John said. That's funny Atkins said, I thought we had.

I've been watching you on the tube and it seems like you're going from bad to worse, when are you gonna stop? Stop! Stop! I just got started. Before I'm done I plan on burning this town down, I'm not leaving a building standing. But 1st I want to see them suffer, suffer just like I've been suffering. Centrale is not going to let that happen John said. I don't think he can stop me, If he could he would have done so. You see I think Centrale fucked up with me, either what he tried on me didn't work or something but I still have what he gave me years ago and I be damn if I'm not going to use it. He can't stop me.

That's where you're wrong Johnny, that's why he sent me, to either stop you or die trying.

Are you willing to risk your life for this town John? I'm not doing it for the town, John said. I'm doing it for me and a debt I owe.

I'm going to do this John and if I have to hurt you in the process I'll do it.

So I can't convince you John said? No, you can't Johnny said. Then the next time we meet we won't be talking like this so all I can say to you is good luck, and John disappeared and reappeared in his hotel room. He walked over to the bar and poured a vodka on ice, called room service and ordered up some lunch. He planned on calling Centrale after lunch and tell him there was no convincing Johnny that he would have to be taken out.

Two days later the town woke up to no transportation anywhere except the two wheel kind and only pedal power. Private automobiles wouldn't start, city buses, nor police cars or taxis. Planes coming and leaving town, aircraft were told to go around. Once vehicles hit the city limits they lost power. Traffic was blocked up for miles even the emergency vehicles couldn't move. Houses burned down because of no fire trucks, people died because of no way to get to the hospital. Babies were born at home, on the street, in taxis. Banks, convenience stores, ATMs, liquor stores were being robbed and the thieves were getting away on bicycles. Marijuana stores were being hit because they held the grass and the money, kind of an all in one stop.

The mayor called his council together a few including the chief of police told him it would be a while before he got there because his kid had the bicycle and he had no other transportation.

The news people were stuck where they were and played hell with going to the bathroom and getting food to eat. Thank goodness the phones came back on but on the good side the take out order people had a booming time, if you could ride a bike and they had them on hand. When the council did get together all they could talk about was how much money the town was losing. Even the feds had to commandeer bikes to get around town. One of the fed's that was in the Council meeting said, let's get real, Atkins is tearing this town apart and we have no counter action for him and I think it's time to give him what he wants. It'll play hell if this thing spreads to the rest of the country.

Are we all in agreement to do this? Do we need to take a vote? I think we can all agree to that, how do we inform him, the mayor said. I'd say face-to-face but how do we get there, the agent said. I've got a feeling he'll come to us the chief said. Let's call him and see.

AFTER ATKINS HUNG up with the mayor he walked over to the bar and poured his self a drink, set down in his lounge chair and started thinking. He told the mayor that he'd be at the Council that afternoon, they decided to give him everything he asked for. He'd listen to what they had to say in essence beg him but his mind was already made up. He intended fucking them any way he could. Maybe he should step outside and informed the media of the meeting and they'll do the rest. Of course they would have a small problem of getting over there, but that's the only way the rest of the world will know what's going on.

11

THE COUNCIL

At four that afternoon the council members were all there in the assembly room waiting for Atkins to show. They were expecting him to come through the main assembly room doors, walked down to the podium and they would address him there. At four instead of coming up the courthouse steps and walking through the assembly doors he just appeared, Right there at the podium. The councilmembers all stood up in amazement! Atkins just stood there until all the commotion calm down and said. I'm here! After the mayor got himself together he addressed Atkins; Mr. Atkins, we've decided to give you what you asked for and to apologize for the death of your daughter. We're sincerely sorry and willing to give you compensation for her death.

We are also willing to give you a pardon for the death of officer Mud Wilder And officer Rankins. We're also willing to forget or overlook the officer's hands you blew off and ones you maze. We're willing to let all those things go if you'll just put the town back to normal. The mayor stopped talking at that point waiting for a reply from Atkins.

Atkins rearranged the Mike so that he was sure they all heard him and that there would be no misunderstanding. And looked at the Council one at a time from left to right.

Gentlemen I think you're all full of shit, you've taken my family my livelihood, kill my daughter and put me in your jail and tried to kill me. Am I supposed to forget all that? No, I don't think so, you have to pay for all that and more. Suffer, just like I've suffered.

 The chief of police jumped up and said. Got damn man, what do you think we been doing these past two weeks. The town has lost enough money where it's going to take us years to replenish. Not to mention the individuals who are not able to get to work, what more do you want?

I won't that and more Atkins said. I won't yo ass!

May I ask when we can expect our transportation to start moving again the mayor said?

I haven't decided Atkins said. I may turn your TV and cell phones off again and you'll have to go back to the old time radio.

You wouldn't do that would you, one of the councilmembers said?

That's only one of the things I can think of, after all I did leave you electric. Atkins said. If you haven't notice it is 98° out there. The hospitals, nursing homes and places like that, what about those? The mayor said.

Fuck the hospitals, fuck the nursing homes, and fuck them all. Did you think of me and mine, hell no you didn't, Atkins said (rising his voice). Gentlemen and ladies, I just started putting a foot up your ass, and then he was gone.

Jamison wrote; if you are asking her what the hell else could happen, you're asking the wrong one. I hear he's talking about cutting off the electric and phones, TV again. It's crazy! The streets are vehicle free, the only thing you see is bikes and skateboards, people walking and jogging. And all the above are in high demand. The phone's, TV and computers are still on for now but please don't cut the electric, I need my AC.

After John talked to Centrale and told him his idea he felt they couldn't wait any longer, true to his word Atkins will tear up this town and according to Centrale he could do it. I agree with your suggestion John and you're right, we can wait no longer, good luck.

John arrived in Atkins front room and spotted him at the window looking out toward the street. Right away he threw a laser beam at him and it knocked him through the window. Atkins laid out on the street and started getting up, the media was recording this and moving back out of the way. The police who were there didn't know what to do. John looked out the window and started climbing out after him, Atkins was on his knees by this time, Saw John and threw a beam toward him missed and hit the window seal above his head. John threw another beam at Atkins and hit him and knocked him into one of the media vans. The media personal scattered and the police started firing at Atkins but forgot if they did that their weapons would explode in their hands and faces. John threw another beam and missed hitting a police car, the police car exploded and lifted in the air. Atkins in turn threw a beam at John hitting him and knocking him 50 feet, he also threw a beam at a police car and media van sending them all in the air and exploding.

After thirty to forty minutes of this it occurred to Atkins that the battle between him and John could possibly go on forever so between brakes in the fighting John came up with a suggestion. Why not leave the planet all together, maybe to an asteroid and do battle there. Only one person would return. Both he and Atkins agreed to this and in the next few moments they were both on an asteroid far above the earth.

Now, Atkins said. That's your ass. I'm going to put something on you that you will never forget and then I'll Return to Lompoc and finished the job there. This is going to be a good day and then I'll move on to the rest of the country.

I don't think so John said. You see the powers that Centrale gave you are only good for as long as you are on earth, once you leave Earth your powers are no longer active. As you can see we are no longer on earth and I don't think Centrale will give it back to you at this point. Unless Centrale has a change of heart this asteroid will be your home from now own. Atkins just looked at John in disbelief, put his left hand up anticipating throwing a beam at him but nothing happened. Then it dawned on him that John and Centrale had tricked him. Had led him like a mule led by a carrot, now he'll never avenge his family on the city and people thereof, and the hate he was feeling.

Johnny, I'm sorry. I'm sorry about everything. Your family, daughter, the whole situation. But I hope you will understand one day that Centrale couldn't let you do what you were doing, I don't know what he has planned for you but I don't imagine you'll be going back to earth anytime soon.

Jamaica:

Damn Centrale you all right, sent me right back to Jamaica to the same beach. Now, if you could just find that same young lady!

Well John, the least I could do for what you did for me and coming up with that asteroid plan, I would have never thought of that, but you did. Don't know where the girl is but if you walk around the beach you may run into her. I'm giving you a week there in Jamaica but after that you'll have to go back in confinement. Look Centrale I'm wasting time, I need to find that little girl, see you in a week.

2 weeks later

2 PM, John was being taken out for his hour in the yard, it's only been two weeks since he's been back but it seems like forever really. Centrale said my replacement did well, of course that's what "it" was supposed to do.

Ismail the guy in the cage next to mine said to me. How did you sleep last night? Sleep last night I said?

Yeah, you remember, you said you wasn't sleeping well. Oh yeah, I said I remember. I slept okay, thanks. How much longer you have left he asked? 3 months 15 days I said.

You not gonna fuck up this time are you john?

Not this time I said. I'm out of here, for real!

JOHN'S RELEASE

John's release:

July 7, 2011 Detroit, Michigan.

HEY JOHN, GLAD to see you out man. How long were you in for?

Long enough dizzy how you been getting on?

Well I don't want to bore you with my problems but things couldn't be worse. The reason why I've been waiting for you...

You been waiting for me dizzy? Why! What can I do for you, how can I help you?

There's a bar across the street, come on and I'll buy you a drink.

Sure, why not.

After taking a booth dizzy asked, what ever happened to that sweet little thing you were dating? Irma, was that her name?

Yeah, John said. She moved on while I was in the joint. She hung in there for as long as she could I guess.

I used to see her from time to time, he said. Then nothing.

You still in the same neighborhood Dizzy, I would have guessed you'd be long gone by now, you were into all kinds of stuff, what happened? Things went from bad to worse John, it'll take more time then you have for me to tell you about it.

What about you John, all those years in the joint and you come right back here, what's the deal?

Look dizzy I'm just here for a minute, just looking around for old times' sake, you lucky you caught me, John said.

Now what's this you need to talk with me about, you know I just got out the place and I don't know a damn thing. Plus all my contacts are gone, I'm surprise to see you still here.

I wouldn't be dizzy said but something went south on me and I don't think I'll ever catch up to it. And what would that be dizzy? I made this hit a few months ago with three other guys and we were supposed to meet up and make the split.

Don't tell me, I said. They didn't show.

Something like that, dizzy said.

What kind of money are we talking about?

240 big ones, dizzy said. My cut was a 4rd of that.

You got any idea what happened to them besides ripping you off?

There was a girl involved, I think she got to one of the guys and he took off with her plus the money and left us high and dry. Two of the guys got into an argument and ended up killing each other. That leaves me hanging out there alone, it ain't right John. I spent six months of my life planning that heist. Six months!

So what do you want me to do dizzy? After the joint I don't want to be sent back over some bullshit.

Nothing like that John, I just need you to help me find these people and my money. I'll be willing to give you 10% of whatever they have left.

Why me dizzy?

Because you're good at finding people John, you always were. And like I said I'm willing to pay.

Have you got any ideas where these people made off to?

Matter of fact I do John, it's a place I once heard them both talking about a number of times.

Well, if you know that why don't you go and collect your money, save yourself 10%.

John, I'm on probation and they won't let me leave town, look here! Dizzy lift up his pants leg and there was on ankle bracelet. So you see, I can't go nowhere.

I asked dizzy why he was on parole and why the ankle bracelets? He informed me it all had something to do with hacking the local banks ATM. We went around collecting the money and they caught on to us, got busted! After that I took up with these other guys, one my friend. And I devised another hit that was a snap, a marijuana store. We hit that place on a Sunday and we were out of there. Besides the money we took some happy smokes, had to take some of that, Check out their products. The reason I picked there is they can't take the money to the bank, it's just lying around their. Smooth! Except when it came time for the split.

Let's say I do fine the people and get the money, you trust me with that kind of money? Dizzy set back in the booth and looked at me and said. One thing you left behind when you went in John was a hell of a reputation. Most people would trust you with their lives, I'm one of those people. I trust you to do what's right, you always have.

All right dizzy, I'll take the job, give me the lowdown on your people and I'll need a little walking around money and if I have to travel, that too.

I got that, Dizzy said.

Since I got nothing better to do, why not take the job. Centrale left me with certain powers the same as he did Atkins but trusting me more so I do have kind of a shield around me and I still have a purpose. Yeah, it's gonna be all right. Nothing wrong with making a few coins along the way.

Dizzy informed me that the two people that I'm supposed to be looking for headed for Fort Lauderdale in Florida. She was still into that Disneyland thing, not too close and not too far away. At 18 where else would you want to be? His old buddy was 28 and they been friends forever but you know how that goes. The nuts always counter friendship. From what dizzy says the girl was some looker, 5 feet 2, hundred and 25 pounds, gorgeous shape and tits larger than a bread basket. Indian and Cuban American descent who always turn heads wherever she goes. His buddy was a short stubby guy of about 5 feet 4 and 200 pounds, head half bald with a full beard. A couple you never think would ever be together, it's got to be the money. Dizzy feels she may have dumped him already.

IRMA'S OLD PLACE, that's why I really come back to see her. I know what Centrale said about she was no longer there but I just wanted to reminisce, just for a minute and then I'll move on and do that little job for dizzy. Another tenant was in the place now but she agreed to let me look around. It took me back to the first time Centrale sent me here and me going to the fridge and getting out some chicken and a bottle of vodka. Her finding me there and we making love for hours underneath the kitchen table. That went on for over a year, then on to Jamaica near the end. Yeah, those were some great times but c'est la vie.

WHAT ARE FRIENDS FOR

In Fort Lauderdale in one of the better hotels I was debating how to handle this search. Centrale didn't leave me with the powers to just pop in on whoever I wanted, Atkins screwed that up. But he did give me the ability to travel to one place or another. Now it's time for leg work. The first thing I did was rent a car and the next I started checking the most high dollar hotels in town. I didn't think Eli, that's Dizzy's friend's name. Would stay any place other than that with the kind of money they had. If I didn't know before I know now, Ft. Lauderdale is a large little city. More hotels than I am willing to admit.

Then I thought, the hell with this. Centrale won't tell me where these people are but he never said anything about transporting myself to the different hotels looking for them, even save on gas and better for the environment. After doing this for a while, even that got tiresome. At the end of the second day I wondered in the lounge/diner having lunch when the paramedics come in and proceeded up to the 5th floor. I finish my lunch and headed out the diner and at the elevator when the other elevator doors open and the medics came down carrying a stretcher. On the stretcher was a body with a sheet covering it, as they were passing John the sheet Slipped Off the body and John saw the face of the deceased? Black male, half bald and full beard. Eli! Could they have been in this hotel all the time? Two days I've wasted and they been here all this time. I asked the medic what room they picked up the deceased. He must have been in a hurry because he didn't ask me any questions just said room 526. In room 526 I walked in and there were two uniform officers, three plane cloths and what look like a couple of CSI people. Before they caught wind of me and ushered me out I heard one of the officers say, whoever stab him got him good, Right Square in the back.

He didn't die right away, he bled out. How long ago doc? At least 24 hours, there was a do not disturb noticed on the door. Also some female articles in the bathroom. We'll have to check with the desk clerk to see if there were anyone else in the room. After answering questions about why I was in that room and what business did I have with the deceased? I told them that I was just nosy and was writing a book. After convincing them I had no business with what was happening they let me go. The girl stabbed Eli in the back for the money, I'm sure of that. You could tell it was a youngster and didn't think things through. It won't take the cops long to put two and two together and come up with the "looker "if she's smart she'll leave town. I figured she has at least 24 hours start, her and the money. Dizzy this is John, just wanted to tell you the latest. Your friend Eli is dead, murdered. Did the girl kill him he said?

I think so, the money is gone to John said. So she is the only one left. Where you headed next, dizzy said?

You said that she loves Disney World, I think I'll head there.

Keep me informed, dizzy said. The next day John was in Orlando a stone's throw away from Disney World. After lunch he started his search of the hotels, at the fifth one he got lucky. He was talking to one of the bell boys and he informed John that he knew of such a girl and he just missed her by two hours or more.

She got on the bus for Disney World, that's the quickest way to travel to avoid a lot of traffic. What's the chances of catching up to her I said? None the bell boy said. You know what it's like out there? Like finding a needle in a haystack.

Well maybe so John said but I have to try.

 Big! That's what I can truly say about Disney World and people on top of people. Kids galore driving me crazy. Since I been in the joint all those years it really took a toll on me. I could use a drink but as you would have guessed no drink could be found, the alcohol type anyway. After a few hours of that I had to get away, the nearest bar would do. Once there I ordered a double vodka, three times. I would have told him to leave the bottle if I could. While I was there since the place had a restaurant I ordered dinner but by that time I was pretty well wasted. Didn't know kids could affect me that way. After dinner I went into the restroom to make the transport to the hotel of the Looker, hoping she was back. I found out her room number and headed for it. At the door I knocked but got no answer, so I knocked again. Still no answer. I looked around for witnesses and then placed my left palm on the lock and it popped open. Walked in the apartment and started looking around. Small kitchen, living room and TV and bar combination. The room had cloths scattered all around like someone went on a shopping spree. I walked into the bedroom and there were more cloths and teddy bears and toys but no looker. I walked into the restroom and there in the bathtub was the Looker or someone I assume was her. White female of about 20 years old, approximately 5 feet 5 and one hundred 20 pounds. Long red hair with a tattoo over her right breast of a Dove. She also had her throat cut from ear to ear. Whoever did it caught her at the right time. The water was red from the blood and look like she hadn't been there long. Too bad! She was a beautiful girl.

I STARTED SEARCHING for the money but nothing, there was a safe in the closet that was open but it was empty. Maybe there was another player in the game I didn't know about? Could she have met someone after she left Eli? There's no other players left that I know of, the only thing I can do now is call dizzy and tell him the latest. Back in my room I made the call. Dizzy, Bad news I said. I found your girl and she's dead, Murdered. Didn't find any money, I guess the person that kill her took it. Damn, I didn't need to hear that John. I guess we're at a dead end now, right? You could say that I said. I don't know where to go from here. Well John, you tried your best, thanks. I owe you.

I'm sorry dizzy, you win some and lose some. There goes your retirement.

Next time John!

The next day I went to lunch and ate at one of those places that has on open air diner where you eat at a table under an umbrella. While I was waiting for my meal a taxi pulled up to the stop light and stopped. I'm just looking around at no one in particular and spotted dizzy in the back of the taxi. My mouth dropped open and I said. What the hell, dizzy! He's supposed to be back in Detroit. The taxi pulled off and I jumped up to follow, there was a taxi at the corner with someone about to get in and I bumped him out the way, got in and told the driver to follow that taxi. The taxi went another two miles and pulled into a small out of the way motel. Dizzy got out and went in, I followed and asked the clerk what room did my friend just go into. Room 256 he said. He just walked in. I know I said, I was with him. Five minutes later I was at the door and in, dizzy was in the restroom washing up. The money was on the bed in bundles. John walked over to the bar and poured his self a vodka over ice, walked back to the bedroom and set down in the chair that was there.

Dizzy came out the restroom and the first person he saw was John sitting in the chair having a drink. John, he said. What you doing here? I should be asking you that dizzy, you're supposed to be in Detroit. Well I, was all dizzy could say.

Dizzy, let me tell you what I think. Looking at the money there I'd say you kill the looker and may have killed your buddy. Did you kill your buddy dizzy?

No, I didn't kill him she did, so I didn't feel anything when I did her. I hated to do it because she was a looker.

How long have you been in town dizzy and how did you find the girl? You led me to her John, what you think. You want to tell me how I did that? I never spotted you following me.

John you been incarcerated a long time, a lot of stuff has happened in that time. Technology! I just hide a tracker on you and I knew where you were all the time. When you call me and told me where you were and where you were going, I just hightailed it over here and to the lookers hotel. So you been here behind me all the time John said?

You could say that John. I was waiting in her room when she got back from Disney World the only problem I had was getting the money out the rooms safe. She did that for me before she took her bath. I was going to let her live but then I thought about Eli and I owe him that much. You should have seen her face when I walked in on her in the tub. What now-dizzy? You got the money, looks like you got away with the lookers death.

What now, Dizzy said? Than he reached under the pillow on the bed and pulled out a 38 caliber revolver and pointed it at John. Well John he said. It's like this. You're the only one who knows about me, you're the only one can take me down.

So you gonna kill me dizzy? You sure that's what you won't to do? I got no choice John, that money there is my future, and by taken you out I've already made 10% on my money.

Dizzy, take your money, less my 10% and walk away.

Fuck you John, then he pull the trigger.

The 38 exploded in Dizzy's hand and took it off, he fail to the floor moaning, John just sit there in the chair drinking his drink and looking at dizzy moaning.

John, got damn help me, help me. Please! The only part of Dizzy's hand that was left was a Stub. Hand gone and blood were all over the bed and floor. John got up and went into the restroom, picked up a towel and brought it back to dizzy. John started picking up the money that was on the bed and putting it in the back pack.

Dizzy just stared at him moaning saying call a medic. I'll tell you what dizzy, I'll bring the phone over to you and you can call the medic yourself.

But my hand is blown off John, I can't call, dizzy said.

You still have another, John said. Try!

Epilogue

Two weeks later John was in Hawaii on the beach, drink in hand and enjoying the evening sunset. Lounge chair and cooler, ladies wearing the usual apparel, close to nothing. A long way from the joint in Michigan, even if Centrale did give me some relief for all that time. Nothing like being on your own. I get to see the sunrise without the bars, the sunset without waiting for midnight when I couldn't leave my cell. No, now I'm good 24 hours a day. The only noise I hear is the ocean and laughing young ladies on the beach. No more screaming all night long and cells opening and closing and occasional suicides. Official intakes every 30 days, guards degrading you every time they pass your cell. No, this is the life! Money, I got it. Permanent R and R (rest and recuperation) I got it. All's good, that is until the next time.

Eddie J. Martin